W9-CKM-089

A ROOKIE READER®

I LOVE FISHING

By Bonnie Dobkin

Illustrations by Tom Dunnington

Prepared under the direction of Robert Hillerich, Ph.D.

CHILDRENS PRESS®

CHICAGO

*For Bryan, my special
fishing buddy*

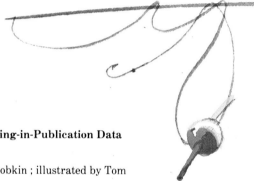

Library of Congress Cataloging-in-Publication Data

Dobkin, Bonnie.
    I love fishing / by Bonnie Dobkin ; illustrated by Tom
Dunnington.
       p.   cm. — (A Rookie reader)
       Summary: A young fisher expresses enthusiasm for
the sport while acknowledging the many potential
. distractions surrounding it.
       ISBN 0-516-02013-7
       [1. Fishing—Fiction. 2. Stories in rhyme.]
    I. Dunnington, Tom, ill. II. Title. III. Series.
    PZ8.3.D634Iab   1993
    [E]—dc20   92-38506
                                                               CIP
                                                                AC

I love fishing!

I watch bugs squiggle.

Feel worms wiggle.

Look for snails.

10

Blow cattails.

Drink my juice.

Chase a goose.

Make mud pies.

18

Catch butterflies.

Pick some flowers.

Play for hours!

24

Sometimes I wish
I'd remember to fish.

27

But I
LOVE
fishing!

WORD LIST

a	flowers	pick
blow	for	pies
bugs	goose	play
but	hours	remember
butterflies	I	snails
catch	I'd	some
cattails	juice	sometimes
chase	look	squiggle
drink	love	to
feel	make	watch
fish	mud	wiggle
fishing	my	wish
		worms

About the Author

Bonnie Dobkin grew up with the last name Bierman in Morton Grove, Illinois. She attended Maine East High School and later received a degree in education from the University of Illinois. A high school teacher for several years, Bonnie eventually moved into educational publishing and now works as an executive editor.

For story ideas, Bonnie relies on her three sons, Bryan, Michael, and Kevin; her husband Jeff, a dentist; and Kelsey, a confused dog of extremely mixed heritage. When not writing, Bonnie focuses on her other interests—music, community theatre, and chocolate.

About the Artist

Tom Dunnington divides his time between book illustrations and wildlife painting. He has done many books for Childrens Press, as well as working on textbooks, and is a regular contributor to "Highlights for Children." Tom lives in Oak Park, Illinois.

JER DOB

Dobkin, Bonnie.

I love fishing.

$17.00

33910031398226
04/06/1999